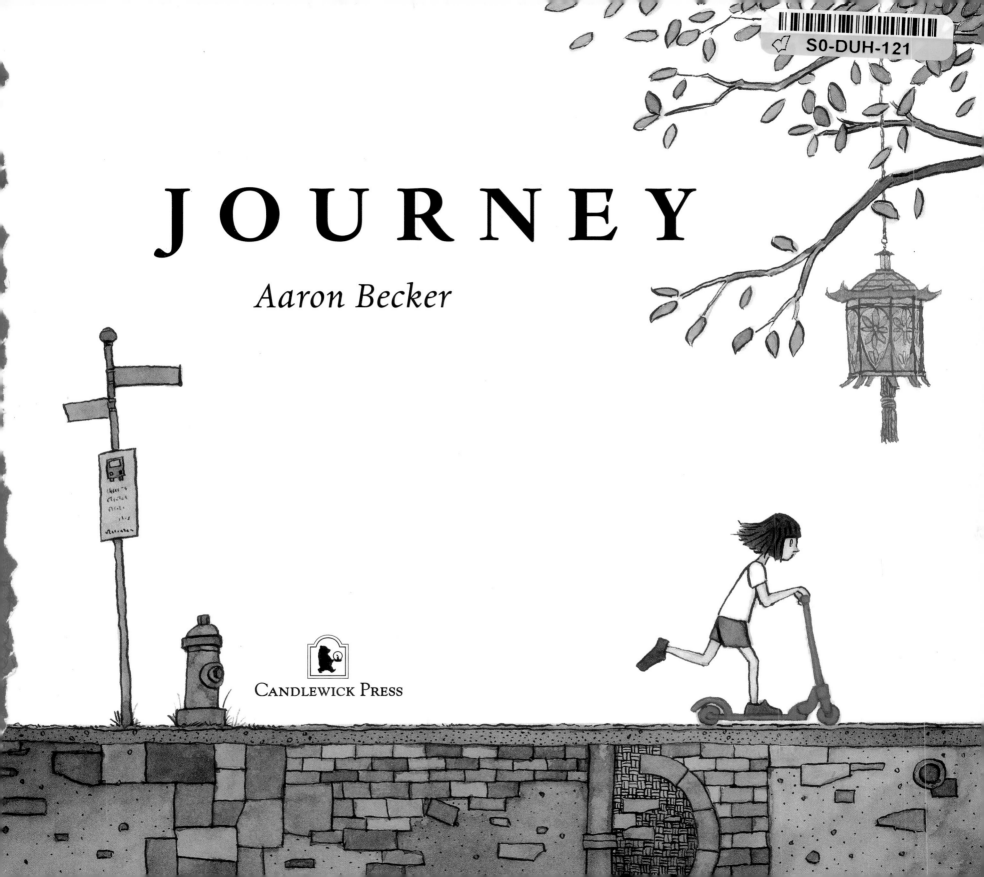

JOURNEY

Aaron Becker

CANDLEWICK PRESS

For Josephine

This book would not have been possible without the help of some great friends and colleagues, notably Joanne Taylor, Laurel Snyder, David Costello, Diane deGroat, Jeff Mack, Linda Pratt, Maryellen Hanley, Mary Lee Donovan, and last but not least, my wife, Darci Palmquist.

First edition 2013

Library of Congress Catalog Card Number 2012947264
ISBN 978-0-7636-6053-6

TLF 18 17 16 15
20 19 18 17 16 15 14

Printed in Dongguan, Guangdong, China

The illustrations were done in watercolor and pen and ink.

Candlewick Press
99 Dover Street
Somerville, Massachusetts 02144

visit us at www.candlewick.com

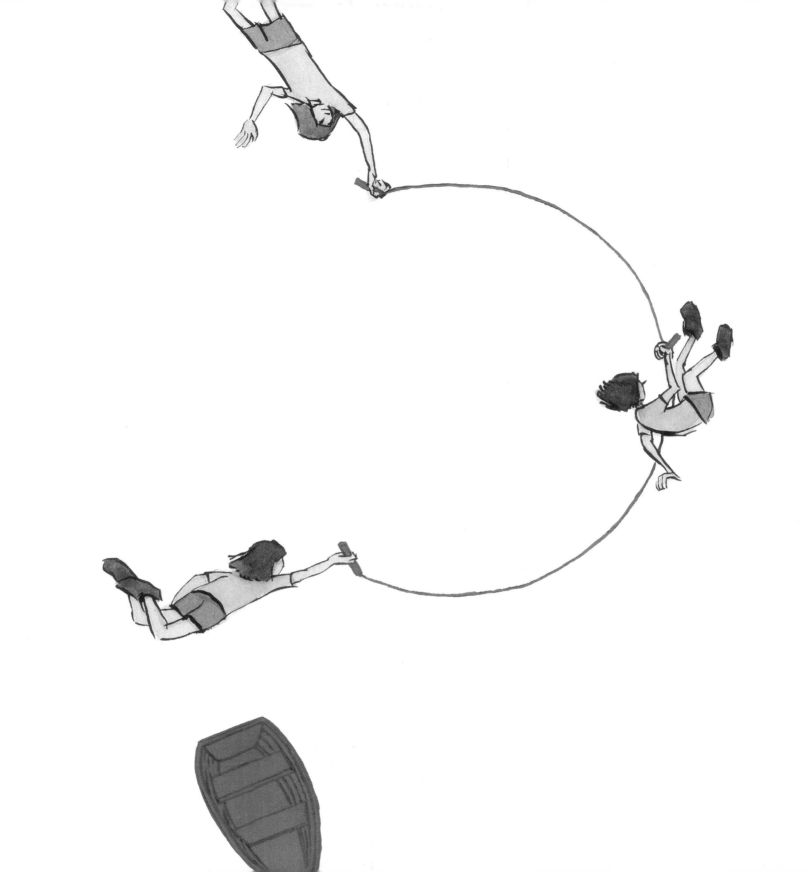